# I WANT TO SAY
## *I Love You*

### CARALYN BUEHNER
pictures by
### JACQUELINE ROGERS

Phyllis Fogelman Books • New York

Published by Phyllis Fogelman Books
An imprint of Penguin Putnam Books for Young Readers
345 Hudson Street
New York, New York 10014

Text copyright © 2001 by Caralyn Buehner
Pictures copyright © 2001 by Jacqueline Rogers
All rights reserved
Designed by Atha Tehon
Text set in Minister Book
Printed in Hong Kong on acid-free paper
1 3 5 7 9 10 8 6 4 2

Library of Congress Cataloging-in-Publication Data
Buehner, Caralyn.
I want to say I love you/Caralyn Buehner;
pictures by Jacqueline Rogers.
p. cm.
Summary: A mother expresses her love for her child
in a humorous way.
ISBN 0-8037-2547-7
[1. Mother and child—Fiction. 2. Stories in rhyme.]
I. Rogers, Jacqueline, ill. II. Title.
PZ8.3.B865 Iaau 2001
[E]—dc21     00-064678

*The art for this book was created with layers of torn and cut paper,*
*penciled in, then painted with acrylic paints,*
*and finally mounted on white paper.*

To my children.
C.B.

For Martha and Emma, with love from Mom.
J.R.

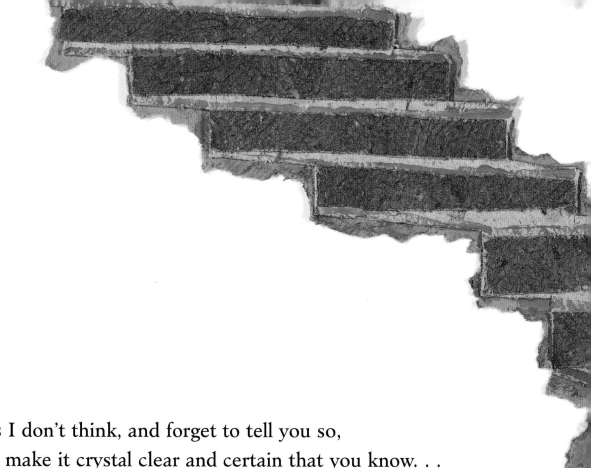

*S*ometimes I don't think, and forget to tell you so,
But I want to make it crystal clear and certain that you know. . .

When I call you to get up and you clatter down the stairs,
With your eyes still blinking sleep, and your porcupine-ish hair,

*I love you.*

When you're ready for the day in your mix-matched sneaker style,
And waiting at the door with bits of breakfast in your smile,
You are beautiful to me.

*I love you.*

And when I see your pictures on the wall, and think back how
I felt when you were small,
I feel the same way now.

You are God's precious gift to me.

When you run from the bus stop when school is out
And come in the door with a bang and a shout,

Let's hug! I'm glad you're home!

You may have wondered if I liked your gift of two dead bees,
Or the "dinosaur skin" that you found around the backyard trees.
I did, because they came from you, and

*I love you.*

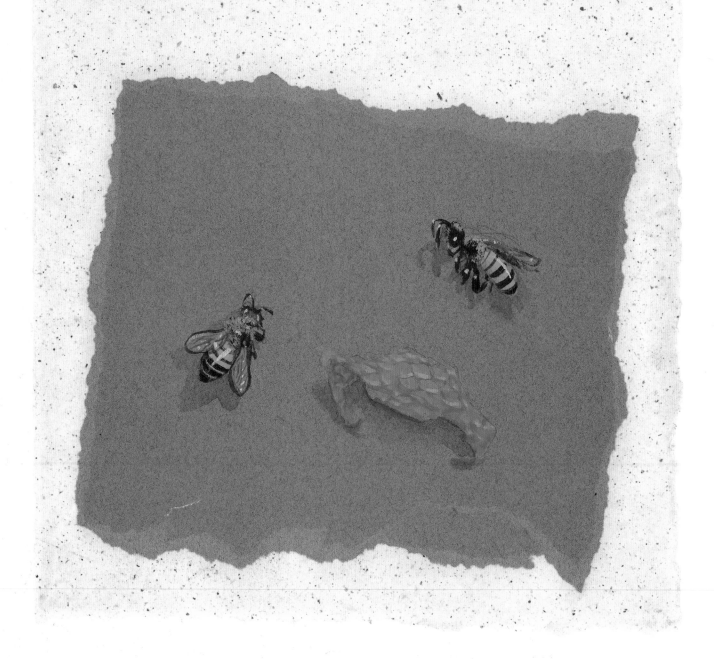

I'm sorry when you scrape your knee falling off your bike.
I remember doing that; I know what it feels like.

I'll help you.

I love to hear you sing with me,
Even on a different key,

I love to hear the things you say,

I love to watch you when you play,

And hold you at the end of day.

*I love you!*

You didn't like it when I took you to the doctor for your shots;

I didn't like it when you colored half the bathroom with blue dots!

I am big, and you're still small,
We don't see things the same at all.

But that's okay.

I watch with wonder how you learn and grow each day,
I marvel at this miracle, and simply want to say—

*I love you.*

*I love you!*